A Grand Old Tree

BY MARY NEWELL DePALMA

ARTHUR A. LEVINE BOOKS
An Imprint of Scholastic Inc.

Library of Congress Cataloging-in-Publication Data

DePalma, Mary Newell.

A grand old tree / by Mary Newell DePalma — 1st ed.   p. cm.

ISBN 0-439-62334-0 — ISBN 0-439-62335-9 (alk. paper)

1. Trees — Juvenile literature. 2. Trees — Ecology — Juvenile literature.

I. Title.   QK475.8.D45 2005   582.16 — dc22   2004023407

10 9 8 7 6 5 4 3 2 1   05 06 07 08 09

Book design by Elizabeth B. Parisi

First edition, September 2005

Printed in Singapore 46

For Pat, Bridget, John, Tom, Mike

and Jean. Love, Mary

Once there was

a grand old tree.

Her roots

sank

deep

into

the

earth,

her arms

reached

high

into

the

sky.

She was home to many creatures.
Birds nested among her branches,

Squirrels scurried through her leaves,
caterpillars and ladybugs crawled about.

The grand old tree

flowered,

bore fruit,

and sowed seeds.

She had many children.

They

changed

the landscape

for

miles

around,

perhaps even

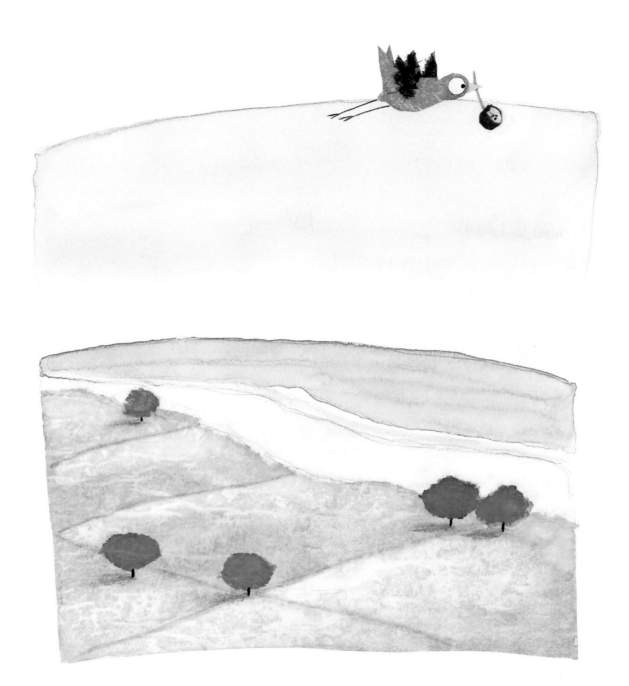

farther than the old tree knew.

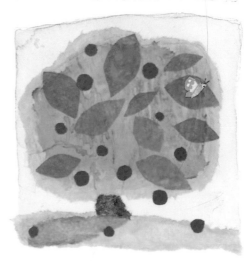

The grand old tree
lived a long, long time.
She basked in the sun,
bathed in the rain,
swayed in the breeze,
and danced
in the wind.

She grew and shed...

...many millions of leaves.

At last, the grand old tree was very, very old.

Her branches no longer
swayed and danced,
but cracked and snapped
in the wind.

Finally she fell,
    and snow gently covered her.

The old tree died.

She no longer flowered,

bore fruit, or sowed seeds,

but she was still

home

to many creatures.

Raccoons nested in her trunk,
centipedes crawled along her branches,
and lichen grew on her bark.

The grand old tree

Slowly

crumbled.

She became part of the earth.

Today the roots of her
grandchildren
sink deep
into
this
earth.
Their arms reach high into the sky.

They are home to many creatures,

just like the
grand
old
tree.